JOSHUA
AND THE BIG WAVE

D1381442

A MACDONALD CHILDREN'S BOOK

Text © Macdonald Children's Books 1989
Illustrations © Rhian Nest James 1989

First published in Great Britain 1989 by
Macdonald Children's Books
Simon & Schuster International Group

Typeset by Keyspools Limited, Warrington
Printed and bound in Belgium by Proost International Book Production

Macdonald Children's Books
Simon & Schuster International Group
Wolsey House, Wolsey Road
Hemel Hempstead HP2 4SS

British Library Cataloguing in Publication Data
Gissing, Vera
    Joshua and the big wave.
    I. Title   II. Nest James, Rhian
    823'.914 (J)
ISBN 0 356 16067 X
ISBN 0 356 16068 8 Pbk

Joshua
AND THE
Big
Wave

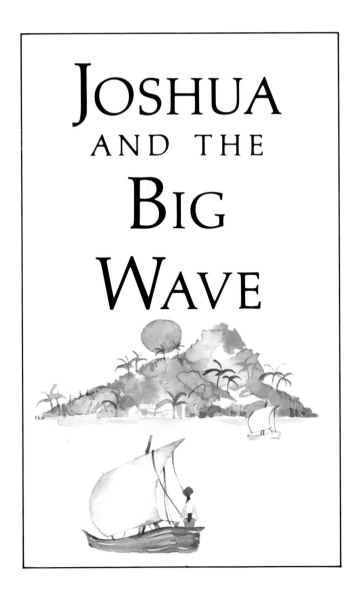

by Vera Gissing

Illustrated by Rhian Nest James

Macdonald Children's Books

There is a little island in the Caribbean Sea with wide golden beaches and high forested mountains. Streams tumble down the slopes to the green valleys below and run like deer across the plains, out towards the sea. The trees are laden with tropical fruit, the grass dotted with exotic flowers. Delicate humming birds hover over the orchids, and bright flocks of parrots and parakeets screech across the sky. The sun shines hot and bright and the rain falls in warm, silver showers.

One day, many years ago, a group of children were playing on the beach. They ran up and down the shore, paddling and splashing in the water. They kept to the shallows, because sharks lurked further out in the deep.

Some of the boys began picking up sea horses trapped in the sand by the outgoing tide, and throwing them back into the water. Others chased barnacle crabs, laughing because they looked so comical as they scuttled away sideways and buried themselves in the sand.

The girls were gathering shells to make ornaments, bracelets and necklaces.

"This must be the most beautiful shell in the world!" cried one of the girls as she ran to her brother. "I can hear the sea singing inside it," she said.

Joshua smiled at his sister. He was a serious boy, a little older than her. He took the white, shining shell from her hand and held it to his ear.

"How strange, Becky," he said. "You hear the sea singing, but I hear the waves crashing and the winds howling. Come on," he added, "let's collect some driftwood for the fire and go home. It must be almost supper-time."

As they strolled, hand in hand, along the beach, the two children came across a strange piece of wood washed up on the shore. A little further on they found the dead body of a beautiful bird that had drowned far out at sea. Joshua stared at the bird and the piece of wood. He suddenly felt worried.

"I don't recognise them at all," he said. "They're not from these islands." He knelt down to the bird, saying, "If you were alive, I would ask: 'Where did you come from? Have you come all the way from China? Did you see the clouds gathering and the winds whipping up the sea, ready to send huge waves towards our island? Have you been sent ahead, together with this strange piece of wood, to warn us that a storm is on its way?' I wish you could tell us!"

He turned to Becky. "I think we should go home and warn the others."

Together they ran inland towards a cluster of straw-roofed huts.

Their grandpa and grandma were sitting in the shade of an umbrella tree. They were old and frail, with skins as wrinkled as dry plums from the many years they had spent working under the hot sun. The children's mother sang as she stirred the big stew pot that stood over the fire.

"There's a big wave coming! I've seen the signs,"
shouted Joshua as the two children ran up. "We've
got to go away at once!"

"What are you talking about? What signs?" said
Grandma.

"We found some wood washed up on the beach,"
Joshua explained. "A foreign piece of wood it was,
not from this island. It looked like Chinese wood.
It's been brought all this way by the sea—sent ahead
by the storm!"

But nobody believed the two children.

"What nonsense, Joshua!" his mother cried. "Why do you always expect bad things to happen? You only have to see a fishing boat come to port and you think that some poor soul has been drowned at sea. Becky here is more likely to think that the boat is filled with treasure for us all to share. She's always full of joy. You're always gloomy. Why can't you be more like her? Cheer up and stop worrying so much."

"I know I'm a worrier," Joshua admitted. "But how *do* you think that piece of wood got to the beach? Do you think that it floated here by itself, or perhaps that it came off a crate in the Chinese market on the big island?"

"That's it!" laughed his grandpa. "You've solved your own puzzle!"

But Joshua was not convinced.

"What about the strange bird we found washed up by the tide?" he went on. "I know every bird on these islands, and this was not one of them. That bird was brought by the sea all the way from China! That's where the big wave is coming from."

"And look what I found," cried Becky, holding up

the pretty shell for all to see. "I can hear the sea singing inside it, but Joshua hears the waves crashing and the wind howling."

"Just like our Joshua!" said his mother, and his grandparents nodded. "Now then, I don't want to hear another word about the big wave! Go and call your father, Becky. He is still out in the fields."

Becky ran to the donkey grazing behind the hut. She planted a kiss on his nose, and then gave his tail a pull. The donkey brayed a loud, clear 'Heehaw! Heehaw!'

It was the family signal to say that supper was ready.

Soon the whole family was seated round the big cooking pot, dipping their cassava bread into the hot stew.

"What do you think, Jacob?" Grandpa asked Joshua's father.

"There isn't a storm cloud in sight," Joshua's father said when he had heard the whole story. "Put away such gloomy thoughts, son, and go to bed."

But Joshua could not sleep. He slid from his hammock, tiptoed out of the hut and wandered down to the beach. The moon had risen, flooding the calm sea in its silver light. The stars hung like glittering candles in the sky and the air was full of dancing fireflies. The tiny waves seemed to be whispering to the sand.

"Are you talking about the big wave?" Joshua asked. He stared out to sea for a while and then walked slowly back home.

Next morning Joshua called his mother outside.
"Look up there," he cried, pointing to a hill path.
"See those goats? They're leaving their pastures and
climbing to higher ground on their own. They don't
know if there will be anything to eat up there, but they
feel in their legs that the big wave is rumbling out in
the ocean, getting nearer and nearer all the time. It
must feel like a lot of carts rumbling up behind them
on a cobbled road."

"Don't be silly, Joshua," said his mother. "Goats don't know anything about the sea!"

"Maybe not," said Joshua. "But they do sense danger. *They* don't want to be swallowed up by a big wave crashing on to these shores!"

But his mother would not listen. Nobody would listen—except for Becky.

"I believe you," Becky whispered and slipped her little hand into his. "But what will the wave do?"

"It will rise out of the sea like a mountain and sweep over the beach, the village and the valley," said Joshua. "There will be a terrible storm with howling winds, thunder and lightning. Everything will be destroyed."

Becky was frightened. "Can't we run away? We could go up into the mountains. If the wave doesn't come we'll come back home again before anyone knows we've gone."

But Joshua didn't want to leave his parents without warning them again. He took a piece of chalk and scribbled a message on the wall. Then he stuffed some bread and fruit into a bag and, taking Becky by the hand, set off up the winding path that led out of the village to the foothills beyond.

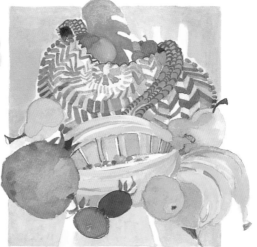

Later that day, a village woman went for a walk along the beach with her children. There, in the backwash from the sea, she saw a peach tree floating, roots and all.

"What a funny-looking tree," said her young son. "And it's got funny fruit."

"It's a Chinese peach tree," said the woman. "It must have fallen off a delivery boat. It couldn't have come all that way on its own."

But even as she spoke she couldn't help wondering whether the tree had been torn from the earth by a storm. She stared out to sea, and noticed some feathery clouds in the distance—a sure sign of a hurricane. She gripped her children's hands tightly, and was suddenly very afraid.

"Joshua was right! There is a big wave coming!" she cried, and hurried back to the village with her children.

At the top of the highest hill on the island, Joshua and Becky waited. They were tired and hungry after their long climb through the dense, steamy forest. They were also lonely and frightened. The sun was setting, the air was still and sticky and the sky was a threatening red. Far out at sea black storm clouds were racing towards the little island.

"The big wave really is coming," whispered Joshua, clutching his sister's hand. "Will we ever see our mother and father, and grandma and grandpa again?"

Suddenly Becky shouted, "Look, Joshua, look!" and she pointed to the path which zigzagged down the mountain.

Joshua rubbed his eyes. He could hardly believe what he saw: a line of people and donkeys were climbing up towards them, their mother and father, grandma and grandpa amongst them!

"You see, Joshua, they did listen to you in the end," Becky said, giving her brother a big hug. "They won't be drowned like that poor bird. We will all be safe up here from the wave."

Joshua and his sister knew that the wave would strike and destroy everything in its path. But, when it had come and gone, they would all be there, alive and safe, ready to begin again.

Joshua put his arm round Becky and waited. He had seen the signs. The big wave had come.

THE AUTHOR

VERA GISSING was born in 1928 in Czechoslovakia where she spent
a happy childhood with her parents and sister. At the beginning
of the German occupation, shortly before her eleventh birthday,
the author was evacuated to England, leaving behind her parents,
family and friends. Her parents later perished during the war.
The diaries she kept as a child during this period form the basis of
Vera Gissing's recently published autobiography *Pearls of Childhood*
which provides a unique record of a young child growing up in an
adopted country. Her career as a writer spans many years
specialising in books for children, writing and translating folk
tales, so that she now has some thirty books to her credit. Vera Gissing
lives in Berkshire and enjoys reading to her grandchildren.

THE ARTIST

RHIAN NEST JAMES was born in the Rhondda Valley in Wales in 1962.
She studied illustration and design at Exeter College of Art and now
works from her studio in Cardiff. A love of vibrant colours which
she feels she shares with most children is characteristic of her
book illustrations and is also found in the artist's landscapes of
her native Wales.

Also in this series:

SAMIK THE BEAR CHILD
by Vera Gissing
Illustrated by Jutta Ash

Abandoned in a snow cave along the bleak, frozen shores
of the Arctic Ocean, Samik the bear cub is taken by
hunters and given to an old Inuit woman to make a tasty
dinner. Instead, Samik becomes her faithful bear 'son'
and the friend and playmate of all the Inuit children.

PRINTED IN BELGIUM BY

INTERNATIONAL BOOK PRODUCTION